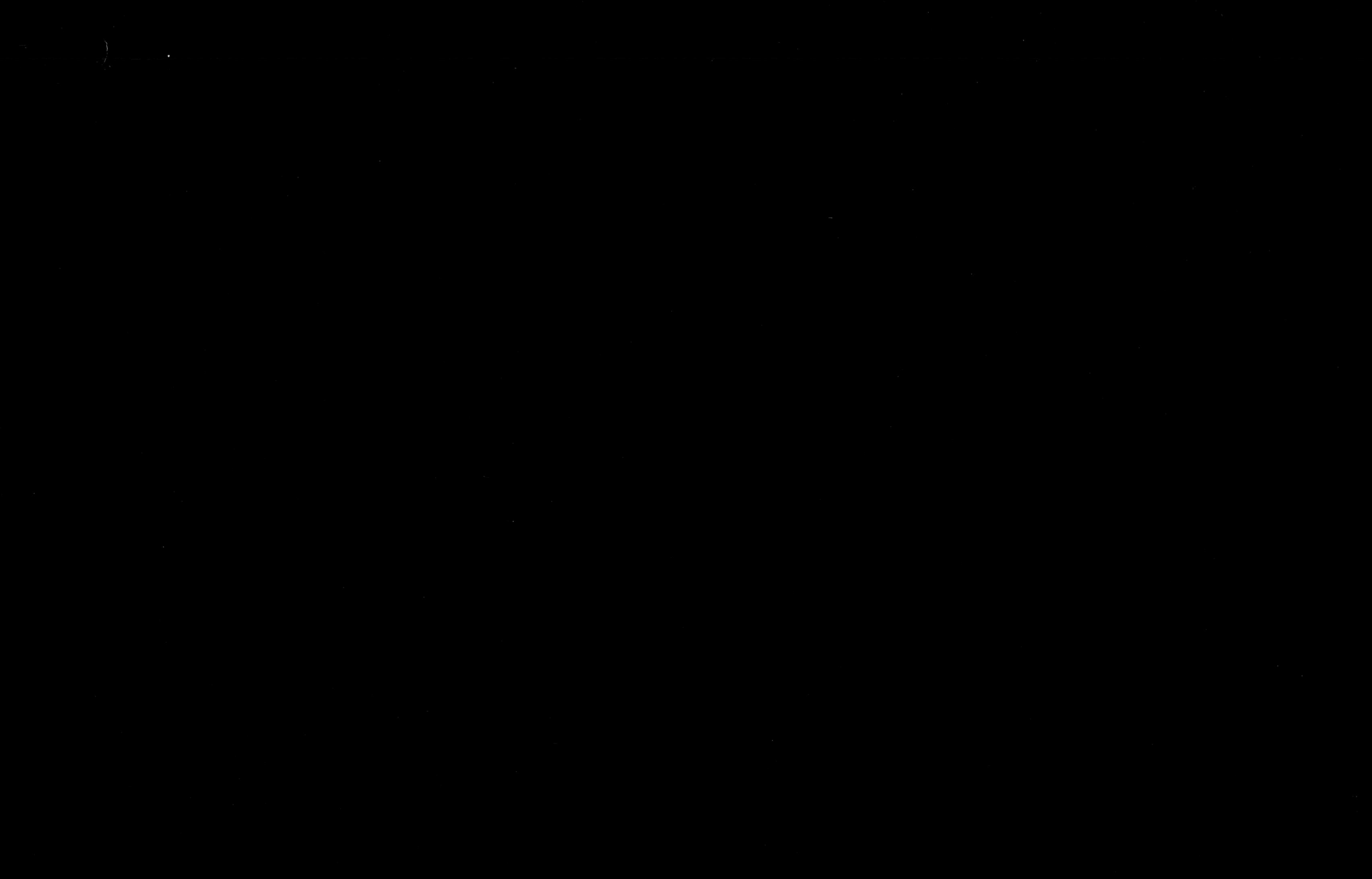

PENGUINS
~~PEOPLE~~
OF AMERICA

Illustrations by James Madsen | Art direction and design by Florence Yue

Little, Brown and Company
Hachette Book Group
1290 Avenue of the Americas, New York, NY 10104
littlebrown.com

First Edition: May 2017

Little, Brown and Company is a division of Hachette Book Group, Inc. The Little, Brown name and logo are trademarks of Hachette Book Group, Inc.

The publisher is not responsible for websites (or their content) that are not owned by the publisher.

The Hachette Speakers Bureau provides a wide range of authors for speaking events. To find out more, go to hachettespeakersbureau.com or call (866) 376-6591.

ISBN 978-0-316-34699-3
LCCN 2016932627

10 9 8 7 6 5 4 3 2 1
IMAGO
Printed in China

ILLUSTRATIONS BY JAMES MADSEN

LITTLE, BROWN AND COMPANY
NEW YORK | BOSTON | LONDON

What are we—sardines?

Aloha, humuhumunukunukuapua'a!

Gentlemen Prefer Penguins

Please...
NO SWIMMING
IN THE TOILETS

Hey, buddy...
keep your eyes on your own flipper!

The big ones are no problem—
it's the little ones that bite.

BINGO

Born to be wild.

I said "Tina." Not "Tuna"!
TUNA

I ordered the mini-jumbo, skinny-nonfat, chocolate-cod, sugar-free, triple-espresso, extra-hot, no-froth decaf.

COFFEE COFFEE

Best.
Summer. Internship.
Ever.

PPER

Why do they call this a catwalk?

BURGER
EMPEROR

Careful, don't waddle
too close to the edge!

Jackson Haddock

Fish Stick

What birdbrain
came up with this?

Of all the icebergs in all the world she had to waddle into mine.

I was way better
at pinball.

Ya know...flippers.

Whoa. It looks like the iceberg is coming right at you!

And to think, just last year this was a polar ice cap.

I told him not to take the red bull!

Remember, R.J.,
lefty-loosey, righty-tighty.

Two, four, six, eight
ice and snow
are really great!

My name is Jason.
I'll be your penguin for tonight.

11
9
2

Is it the Polar Local?

Or the Polar Express?

FREEZE!

OMG I love Jimmy Shoe's
new mukluks!!!!!

It ain’t over till the fat penguin sings.

FASHION
TAKA
WEBBE

I sure hope our hotel
has blackout shades.

The real challenge is getting
the quarters in the slot machine.

Shake, waddle, and roll.

Sometimes you've got to go against the floe.

"One for the money, two for the snow."

387
387

Aye, McBird here was the first golfer
to complete a subzero round.

I should wax my what?

If we leave now, we'll only be *two* hours late.

Relax. It's just my cousins from Greenland.

Catch of the day.
44

The first triple-Salchow backside-quadruple-rodeo belly flop.

They make terrible pets.
TEEN

CAJUN
They call me Bird.

LOVE BIRDS
YOU
ME
YOU WILL MEET YOUR MATE TODAY
Bliss
Mr & Mrs
XO

I DO
let the journey begin

Hurry up, Harold.
The all-you-can-eat fish fry
starts in ten minutes.

As the sun sets slowly in the west we bid you a fond ee-hee-aw haw, ee-hee-aw haw, ee-hee-aw haw-ay!

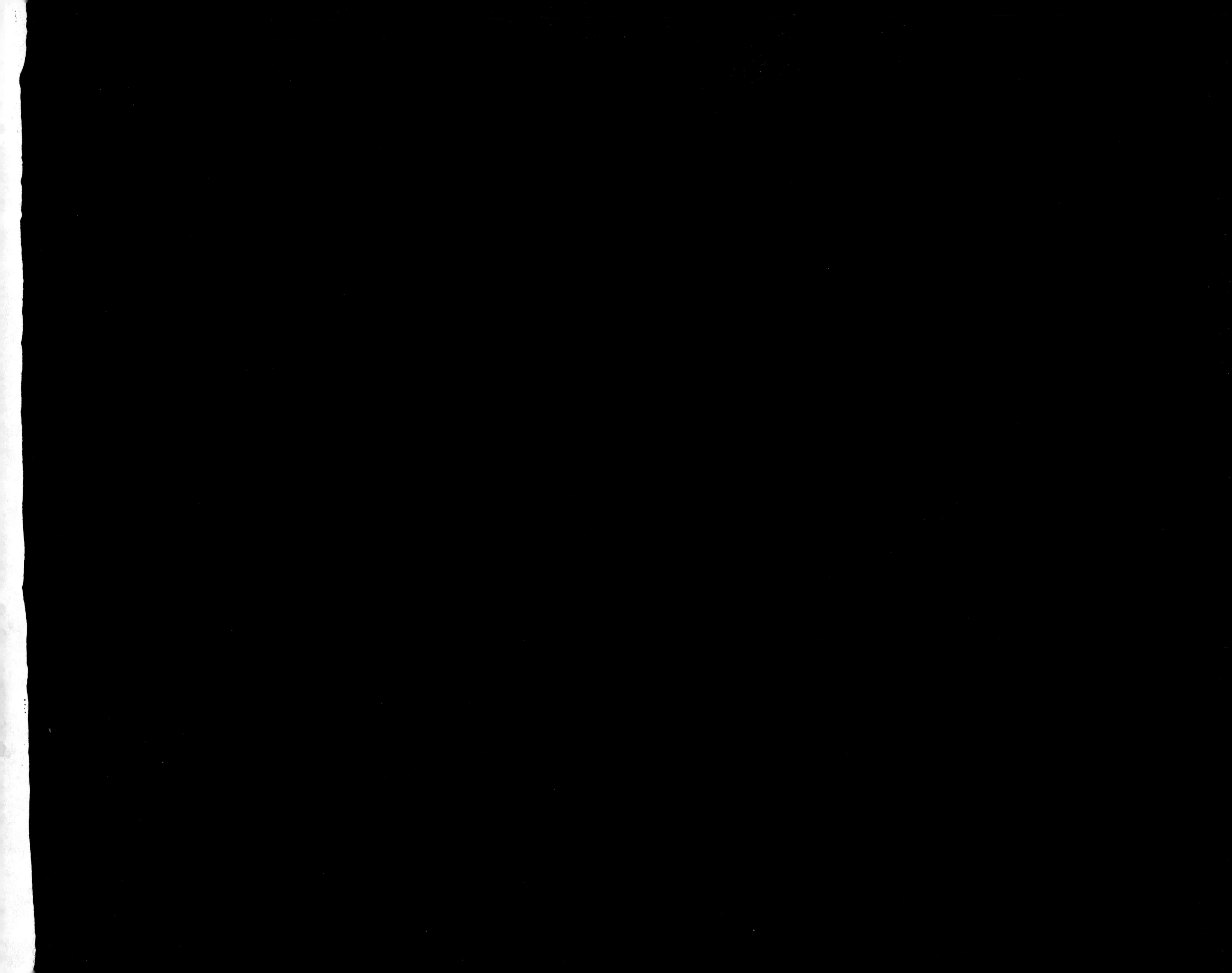